Mesha
The Mistress

Lica Marks

ISBN: 0-9989661-0-X
ISBN-13: 978-0-9989661-0-6

DEDICATION

This book is dedicated to all the women out here trying to find a good man. To the mistresses that love their titles and to the wives who hate mistresses. There is truly someone for everyone, women are not here to be treated like dogs. No man should define any women. Women are capable of doing amazing things in life, but we need to monitor what we do with our bodies. Our sexuality is alluring, however; we should learn to save that talent we have for a special man. Married man are not your special man, they are married! That being said, just because you fall for one married man doesn't mean you have to continue with that pattern. You are able to redeem yourselves , move -on with your lives. You don't have to look for love, love will find you.

CONTENTS

ACKNOWLEDGMENTS

All praises to my Lord and Savior! God I don't know what I would do without you. You are here for me when no one else is. I just want to thank you for all you have done for me..

CHAPTER 1

PRESENT DAY

Mesha: Today is a new day, I can't change the person I was yesterday, but I can manage the person I will become. Yes, every day I wake up and look in the mirror, I chant these words." I'm working on building my self-esteem and holding myself accountable for the trifling things I've done in my life. I am worthy of my own man and I am willing to wait. "You would think a girl shouldn't need to chant affirmations, after all, doesn't everyone already love themselves enough to want a man of their own, I mean, tell me no one is really purposely setting themselves up for failure? Well, I thought I knew what was good for me, thought I had my life altogether. But after all the shit I've been through and the mess I've made of not only my life but the lives of many other women, I had a harsh reality check that told me very clearly, I didn't love myself at all! I gave my body freely to any man who talked that talk, without even requiring him to wife me, or at least friend me. Let me see if I can get you caught up! Trust

me you won't believe this hot ass mess, but stay with me!

CHAPTER 2

BACK THEN

Six years ago, on March 26th, 2010, my 26th birthday, I was out with my bestie, Tina and some of her coworkers. Tina was four years older than me and a partner at People, Walker & Watkins, so I was sure she would never take me to some trashy nightclub, she was sophisticated and prided herself on partaking in nothing but the best! Tina insisted on taking me to this new club downtown Indianapolis, I wasn't really feeling it at first. I never went downtown for anything! Once we got there, Tina starts telling me this place is not what I would expect in a club, so just give it a chance. I just looked at her and thought, this bitch better not have me at a lesbian nightclub on a night that she knows I need some dick. To my surprise, we enter a hotel and take the elevator to the top floor. When the doors opened, the view of the city damn near stole my breath. While I stood there in awe of such amazing beauty, Tina's co-workers went in one direction and Tina went in the other, saying she'll be right back. I took two steps back trying to sidestep a waitress and fell into a chair. I looked around to see if anyone noticed me stumble when I felt the chair move. I slowly turned to find brown eyes steering into my soul! OMG, I said trying to stand up. I'm so sorry, I didn't mean to, OMG! I was so embarrassed I almost tripped over my own two feet trying to get out of sight. The only problem was, this man had still not let go of my waist. He turned me to face him and he immediately embraced me. I'd just met the man of my dreams! Gavin was 6-foot 6inches tall, milk chocolate skin tone, super thick biceps, sexy brown eyes, and a size 14 shoe! Yes, I did say size 14. Once I'd recomposed myself, Gavin asked me to have a drink with him. One drink led to 4 glasses of white wine, two glasses of water and half a dozen oysters on the half shell. By the second glass of wine, I knew his full name, Gavin Demarcus Deleon, age 29, Owner of Deleon Advertising and Marketing firm. By the 4th glass of wine, Both Gavin and I had loosened up and were talking like we were two old friends. I'd been out of contact with my girl but I didn't mind until I heard the last call at the bar. Damn, where in the hell is Tina? If she doesn't come soon I'm leaving with Gavin. My bestie must be a mind reader, cause as soon as I had the thought of doing me tonight, this chick pops-up out of nowhere asking if I was ready. Slightly disappointed I gave

Gavin one last hug and strolled to the door with Tina.

Gavin: Mesha was a pretty cool chick! I think I'll call her tomorrow

and see if we can hook-up. If her girl hadn't come back, she was

going home with me. I was ready for some action too, after all those

oysters and drinks, shit I was ready! Good thing I ran into Jalisa while

waiting for my Uber. Jalisa is a chick I used to smash back in the day.

She was looking like she could get it. I asked her if she needed a ride

when my Uber came, I opened the door to let Jalisa in first, next

thing I knew she was on her knees in front of me with my dick

halfway down her throat, I still had my door keys in my hand! I

forgot how freaky this chick was. After I'd cum in her mouth, she

made a show of swallowing it, stripped down naked, and walked to

my bathroom. I didn't move right away, I was drained and needed a

minute or two. I heard the shower and managed to get to my feet, I

glanced down at my dick still limp it started to tingle. I made it to my

room where I took all my clothes off and opened my nightstand

drawer, oh shit no condoms! No, I'd just purchased two boxes. I go

to my closet top shelf and pulled out the brown box that had been

delivered just yesterday. Bingo! Two boxes, 50 condoms in each. I grab a box, removed 4 condoms, placed 3 in my nightstand drawer, and kept one with me. When I opened the bathroom door I had a full view of Jalisa sucking her own breast and sliding her finger inside her pussy. I could feel my dick growing, I put the condom on and almost broke my glass shower door trying to get in. I took Jalisa's other breast and sucked her nipple, I grabbed her butt and separated her cheeks running my index finger around her anus, I picked her up and set down on my built-in shower bench. She screamed when I dropped her on my dick! I didn't give a fuck, I just kept grinding her pussy. She was acting like I put it in her ass! She jumped up as soon as I loosened my hands. I thought she was leaving but to my surprise, she turned the hot water up and bent over in front of me, when I didn't move she looked back at me and slapped her ass, and spread her cheeks. I jumped up and put my dick on the spot just to make sure we were on the same page. She said come on, give me that dick! I plunged in, she grunted and started grinding her ass back on my dick to meet every stroke. That ass was so tight, I busted fast and she knew it. I slid out of her and she turned, took the condom off put it in the trash just outside my shower. Came back and washed her body then turned to finish washing me. I was weak and couldn't really stand. When she was done cleaning my body she rinsed me off and turned the water off, grabbed a towel and dried me, she walked with me to my bed where we fell asleep no sooner than our heads hit the pillows. It seems like I'd just gotten to sleep when I felt something warm and wet on my manhood. I felt my penis getting hard. I was tired as hell but I knew she was a freak, so I grabbed a condom out of the nightstand and handled that ass! What's crazy is that I kept wishing Jalisa was Mesha. Jalisa's sex was good, but she talked way too reckless for me, she could never be my number one.

Mesha: I'd awaken to the smell of something sweet in the air. Confused about where I was, sitting up I noticed the sun shining through the sheer blue curtains that hung from the Hexagon shaped window. Tina's house was stunning! Each room was beautifully decorated with different colors. I was in her downstairs guestroom, right across from Tina's luxurious master suite. After leaving the club last night, I told Tina I would just stay at her place and she could take me home after church. I keep spare clothes at her place, and she does the same at mine. Most times we'd shop together and send our new items to each other's house. Looks like today might be one of our shopping days since church starts at 10:00 am and it is now a quarter till 11. I slowly rolled out of bed and went into the bathroom to relieve myself. Once I handled my business, I strolled into the kitchen where Tina had just finished cooking chicken sausage patties. I looked around as I spoke to my friend. Wow, girl, this looks good, she handed me a plate and I immediately put one of the crepes on my plate, this was the sweet smell that woke me up. I didn't want to seem greedy but I was hungry as hell, I'd eaten half the crepe before I'd finish loading my plate with eggs, chicken sausage, and Homestyle potatoes. Tina was a great cook! I love when she makes crepes!

Tina: By the time I woke up this morning It was clear to me that there'd be no morning service today. I was extremely hungry so I decided to fix a nice breakfast for Mesha and I. It's a good thing I'd cooked, I thought I was hungry, but Mesha almost devoured a whole crepe before sitting down. Here, girl, I said bringing the platter of crepes over to the table. I know we're going shopping today after this big breakfast, we both need to work some of this food off. Once we'd both stuffed ourselves, we went back to our rooms to get showered and dressed so we could get ready to shop. I needed more shoes, I'm thinking a pair of black stiletto's, something with an ankle strap. I might need to take a little nap first.

CHAPTER 3

THE BEGINNING OF THE END

Gavin: Mesha, it's Gavin from the club Saturday night. Listen I just want to know if you'd like to go to dinner tomorrow night?

Give me a call at 317-555-5252.

"I'm going to make Mesha mine!"

Mesha: After checking my voice mail I did return Gavin's call and accepted his dinner invitation, who knew he would turn out to be the best and worst man I'd ever meet.

Gavin was wonderful, he did things for me and to me that no other man had ever done like rubbed my feet, washed my hair, suck and licked every part of my body without being asked. He never worried about reciprocation. Things were going great, then he had to go away on business. When he came back he became somewhat hard to reach, however that didn't give me pause. He started coming over to my place a lot and I thought it was kind of nice having him around, but one day I came home to a note on my dining room table. It was Gavin's handwriting so I sat down my purse and briefcase, picked up the letter and read it.

The Letter:

Dear Mesha,

By the time you read this letter I will be married. I know you thought we'd be getting married, but I didn't have the heart to tell you I couldn't marry you. Remember that business trip I took a few months ago? Well, the meeting took place in Turks and Caicos; it was there where I met my wife Tamia. I knew it from the moment I saw her, she was the one, so I proposed onsite. Today we got married. Mesha, I am truly sorry if you feel I wasted your time, you are a beautiful woman and someday you will find the love you deserve.

PS: Maybe we can still be friends if you're open to it. Please don't stay mad at me, I never meant to hurt you.

With Love,

Gavin

Mesha: I stood there holding that letter with tears rolling down my face, I wanted to call him but I figured he would've had his number changed. I could call him at work, only he wouldn't be in for a couple of weeks at least. I balled the letter up in a rage and went to my bedroom. He'd taken all his things right down to the toothbrush like he was trying to erase himself from my life. I must've cried myself to sleep because I woke up on the closet floor when I heard my cell ring. Dazed, I didn't remember where I'd left my phone. I struggle to get up off the floor. Looking around trying to find both my phone and a clock, I made it to the kitchen, my phone had stopped ringing by then. Ding Dong, Ding Dong. Great, now someone was at my door, I'm sure I looked a mess, I finally spotted a clock on my stove. 9:45 am. I'd fallen asleep and slept on my closet floor all night. How pathetic is that? Now someone was ringing my doorbell and trying to knock down my damn door. I snatched my front door open to an angry face.

CHAPTER 4

GET OVER IT

Tina: Girl I've been calling you for an hour, I'm on my way over to your house and you had better be ready for church. I pressed end to hang up my cell and drove to Mesha's house. Now I'm at the front door ringing her bell like a mad man. Mesha answers the door looking like hell warmed up and worked over. I don't know what's wrong with her, but I know we're not going to make morning service this Sunday. What happened? I asked but before she could get anything out, I walked to her room and entered her humongous bathroom, dropped the drain in the big soaker tub, turned the water on, and poured some lavender bath oil in with two scoops of Epson salt. I then turned to my friend who looked so pitiful and helped her undress and get into the bath. While she soaked I excused myself and went to her guest bedroom, walked into the closet, and selected leggings and an oversized tunic with a pair of slip-ons. I was ready to get answers from my friend and I know by now she'd be ready to talk.

Mesha: I was miserable. For days and then weeks I didn't want

anyone to see me. Of course, Tina always made herself known and

tried to help me out in every way possible, but seriously I was

devastated. Gavin had taken my heart out, ripped it to shreds, and

then tried to glue it back together. He wanted to be friends? Hell

no…I did not want to be friends with him. I wanted to hate him and

I really did. I didn't think I would ever get rid of that hatred for him,

but then I met Tyrone. I didn't look for it and I had no intention of

seeking out another man, but Tyrone was just there. I walked into

the grocery store and it was like our eyes just met and we both knew

instantly, we were going to find a way to be together. It didn't

happen right away…in fact, I didn't think it would ever happen, but

then I ran into him again and I mean literally. I was walking out of

the restaurant and he was walking in. I bumped right into him and

bounced off his hard chest. We laughed and as I tried to steady

myself, I said, excuse me. It was then that I realized that this was

Tyrone. Tyrone? I asked in utter disbelief. He snickered. We were both shocked to be seeing one another, especially after I had put it out of my mind that we wouldn't see each other again. We knew we had to exchange numbers and that night my phone rang and it was him. He invited me out to a club the next night and I couldn't wait to see him. My thoughts were that suddenly my dreams would come true and I wanted nothing more than to see Tyrone. Okay, maybe I wanted a little more. I wanted to have dirty sex with him. I was not ashamed of where my mind would go.

Tyrone: When I ran into Mesha, not once but twice, I had to find a way to go out with her. I wasn't the least bit surprised when she claimed she wanted the same. We met at the club and it was instant chemistry. I found myself laughing with her as if I was a teenager. She was beautiful and sexy and nothing else seemed to matter when I was with her. So, after we had a bite to eat, we hit the dance floor. I'll be honest that girl had some moves. I was panting to keep up with her me, the King of Dance. So, I was impressed. My eyes trailed over her body as she danced and then I pulled her to me. My dick was so swollen that it was only a matter of time before I had to have her. I could only imagine the mess I'd have in my underwear if I didn't. So, I leaned against her ear and whispered, wanna get out of

16

here? She anxiously agreed and we took off. We got out into the cool air and I turned her around and pulled her to me. My mouth went to hers and we kissed right outside the club doors. I need you so much right now, my dick is calling your name, I mumbled. I could see her smiling at my words and we parted from the kiss. I took her hand in mine and we begin running towards the hotel next door. We got inside and I paid for the room for the night. The hotel employee didn't even question that we had no luggage, my heart was racing. We hurriedly made our way through the lobby and to the elevator. Once in the elevator, I pushed her against the wall and started kissing her. My tongue was so far down her throat that it was amazing she didn't start choking. *Ooh, no gag reflex* great-! Her lips tasted like sweet heaven and I wanted more of it. The elevator door opened and we stepped out, then ran to our room. This was going to be one night I wouldn't soon forget.

CHAPTER 5

WHAT'S NEXT?

Mesha: Let me tell you a little about Tyrone. As we got into the hotel room, I really had a chance to admire his features. As each piece of clothing fell to the floor, I noticed his biceps, triceps, abs, and …OMG, his freakin' HOT ass. I grabbed onto his ass and we wandered over to the bed. He was deep brown chocolate, with a smile that melted my heart. And all the features that I mentioned, his biceps, triceps, abs, and ass were on point and sexy as hell. My hands were groping him so fast because I didn't want to miss a single inch of this man I was about to have heated sex with. My pussy was on fire and throbbing as we rolled around on top of the bed, kissing, and rubbing! His dick was so swollen and rubbing alongside my thigh it had me begging for him. He rolled on top of me and I could feel the tip of his dick at my entrance. It was almost too late, as I gasped for him to get a condom. Then I had utter panic that maybe he didn't bring a condom, but I need not have worried because he crawled off me and reached for his pants pocket. I was breathing heavy and waiting for him. My body tingled from head to toe as I couldn't stand the wait. He finally came back with his condom on and we resumed places. I spread' my legs and he slid effortlessly inside of me, plunging into my deepest place. I screamed out with pleasure as his balls slapped my ass and his dick plowed further into my sweet abyss. I took him all in as his lips went back to mine and I felt his large hands groping my even larger breasts. In and out...in and out...we were moaning and groaning and he was thrashing hard against me. When my orgasm reached me, I had to hold onto him as I shook and seized beneath him. He collapsed on top of me and we remained locked in a hold, never wanting to let each other go. I felt this connection that had been missing since Gavin and I split, so I was ready for Tyrone to take his place. Little did I know...Tyrone was ready to disappoint me, leaving me heartbroken once more.

Tyrone: I didn't know how it happened. One minute I'm flirting relentlessly with Mesha and the next minute I'm going out with her, having sex with her, and then falling into a relationship with her.

Don't get me wrong, when I looked at Mesha, I saw simple perfection, so in my right mind, I would say, yay to me. I scored the sexy woman. However, there was a lot of heartbreak that could go with that little thought and I really had to discuss that with her. So, after a few weeks of really getting to know Mesha and one steamy night of sex, I decided to take the plunge. I need to tell you something, I started. She seemed eager to hear what I had to say, even though I wasn't as eager to tell her. I took a deep breath and just confessed everything. I'm married, I blurted out. She laughed and it was pretty obvious she didn't believe me. I had to explain quickly before I really lost my nerve. I'm being serious here, I told her. I told her that I knew it didn't make sense, because of all the times we'd been together, but my wife was frequently out of town for business and it made things easier. Her response was nothing short of get the hell out of my bed and in an instant, it was over.

CHAPTER 6

MESHA THE MISTRESS

Mesha: Maybe I wouldn't have been so upset if I hadn't experienced the same thing with Gavin. My God, did I have two-bit whore written on my face? Did all the married guys think that I wanted to have affairs to break up their marriages? I was stunned when Tyrone honestly thought I would be okay with it. He wanted to continue our relationship and I, in no uncertain terms, told him to get lost. I couldn't possibly picture having a relationship with him when he spent weeks lying to me. Okay, I'm no saint and it is possible and even probable that had Tyrone explained to me from the get go, then I probably would have been more open to it. Hell, he was hot. So, it was very likely that I would have thought nothing of fucking him and just letting the chips fall where they might. I actually felt a little sick thinking about that, but it was done and over with and Tyrone was out of the picture. But that didn't stop me from thinking about getting on with my life and figuring out how I could do that when it seemed like my love life was non-existent. So, when my friend Donna mentioned she was going out on the hunt for men, I was all for it. You would have thought that I'd learned my lesson, right? Not even close. My love life only got stranger from there.

CHAPTER 7

BACK IN THE GAME

Donna: I stood outside Mesha's house, pounding on her door. When she didn't come, I yelled out her name. Finally, after ten minutes of handling this charade, she came to the door. I looked at her. She wasn't dressed, but her hair had been curled. Get your lazy ass dressed, I said, bursting through the door. She frowned at me and gave me this whiney ass excuse that there was no point and who needed men, blah blah blah. I wasn't buying any of it. I knew Mesha. Mesha was nothing without a man by her side and I could tell that depression had completely taken control of her actions. Come on! I called, hoping she would follow me. We're going to find something hot and sexy for you to wear. She grumbled behind me, but I didn't stop until I had rummaged through her entire wardrobe and pulled out a black silk dress, and black high heels that would have men falling all over her. I was going to get her laid if it was the last thing I did.

Mesha: I got dressed, but let me just tell you that it took a lot of effort. Here's the thing, thoughts kept parading my mind of how much I wanted this too. I wanted to have another dick to devour! I wanted to be with another man and be brought to the highest of orgasms. I wanted to have someone cherish me, as past men in my life had at some point. I just didn't want this man to be married. I didn't think that was too much to ask for. So, I got dressed and we left my place and headed to the club. The whole way, Donna was excitedly talking about how she couldn't wait to have her night. She'd been single a lot longer than I had, so I was sure she was worried that her pussy was all dried up. But I was still contemplating how I wanted the evening to go. I missed Gavin. Damn, why did things have to be so complicated? Donna turned into the parking lot of the club and it was already packed. We headed up to the doors and went inside. The smoky atmosphere immediately hit me. I started coughing and Donna just rolled her eyes at me. We went to the bar and ordered our drinks and that's when things went awry. Donna immediately took off with some dude in a J. Benzal suit and a thick mustache. I opened my mouth to argue with her and tell her she forced me to come out when I spotted him. He walked over to the bar and took a seat next to me. My head was spinning with the smell of his cologne. I turned back around and stared ahead, wondering if he would know how much he had me, without even saying hello. My knees were shaking and I slowly took a drink of my wine. I didn't even think he noticed me until I heard him speaking and he said hello. I grew nervous and greeted him with a high-pitched voice. Hello? It came out more in a form of a question. He started laughing and in that moment, I relaxed. I took a deep breath and I just pretended like nothing never went wrong in my life. Yes…that was the biggest joke of all but he didn't need to know that.

CHAPTER 8

SEEMS TOO GOOD

Javon: The moment I sat down, I knew I had to speak to her. Her body radiated heat up my spinal column. Hello, I said. She briefly responded with the same, but it was like she was so nervous that she didn't know what to say. I liked that. It made me feel like I was in control of the situation. We talked for a minute. She told me her name and I said that I thought Mesha was a beautiful name. I then said, my name's Javon! Her face lit up and just let the conversation flow. When we finished our drink and I invited her onto the dance floor, she got close up. She told me that she didn't feel comfortable because she wasn't a good dancer, but I had to set her at ease. I told her that I won the worst dancer award three years straight and she laughed at that. She was putty in my hands. We went out to the floor, but I had to tell her right away that she was wrong. She was one of the best dancers I had the privilege of dancing with. She blushed in my arms and I held her close. We were getting closer the later it got and I was getting hornier the later it got. I knew that to approach the subject, could be the death of this thing we had, but I needed to at least try. You know, I think we should get out of here and find someplace more intimate. Do you agree? I asked. She looked up at me. The longing was in her eyes, but she still seemed apprehensive. I had to tread lightly, but there was just something about her.

Mesha: I couldn't remember the last time I'd had so much fun. Well, that was a lie, because it was when I was with Tyrone, but Javon seemed like another catch that I was ready to reel in. There was only one thing that I had to ask before I could fully commit to hooking up with him. Are you married? I asked. I just had to ask, like I was pulling off a band-aid. His face was as white as a sheet and I thought, *Shit…he is.* I started to tell him to forget it. I already had too much going on in those scenarios. He stopped me from leaving and he explained why he seemed surprised by my question. He was going through a divorce and he had been out of love with his wife for a while, so in his mind he was single. It sounded like bullshit and something that he figured I just wanted to hear. Yet, I fell for it…hook, line, and sinker. We were out of the club and seeking out a more intimate place, as he put it. That intimate place was his car. We were pulling off our clothes before we even got seated in the backseat. Once my pussy was revealed, he started fingering me, running his fingers deep into my folds and massaging with intense strokes. I was groaning and grinding against his fingers as my mouth went to his. We kissed, with his tongue thrashing against mine. My body moved in time with his swipes and I bounced on top of his fingers while his other hand stroked and pinched my nipples. When I clenched onto his fingers, I started squirting all over him and he was exuberantly moving his fingers around my juices. He slid out of me and grabbed onto my waist, then lowered me down to his seat in the back. I didn't realize how roomy it would be. We were going at it, kissing and grinding one another and I felt his dick as stiff as a board. I don't even know when he had time to sheath himself, but soon he had a condom on and was opening me up, literally splitting my insides. I bucked up and bit back a scream and then had to force myself to relax. He set into a smooth ride and we just went back to kissing and letting ourselves be in the moment. I didn't want to let go.

Javon: When I was with Mesha it was like the world stopped. Every time I had the chance, I was meeting up with her. We had been pretty hot and heavy for a month when I felt the urge arise again one night and I had to be with her. I texted her and told her I was coming to her place. She said she couldn't wait to see me, so I got ready and was about to leave the bathroom when I saw Jennifer, my wife standing at the door. She had on a sexy negligee, one that screamed she was ready to get fucked. I looked her over and the thing that hit me was I wasn't aroused. I tried pushing past her but to my surprise, she became aggressive unzipped my pants and dropped down to her knees. She sucked my dick so good I damn near fainted! She pushed me to the chair in the corner of our bedroom and straddled me, her pussy was so wet I couldn't believe this was my wife. She had never sucked my dick like that before and she had definitely never taken the dick so aggressively. What the hell was going on. After I busted a nut I jumped in the shower, she took a bath. I'm going out, I said. She huffed, irritated that I completely ignored her plea to keep me home. She wanted to know where I was going and I had to lie. I turned around and looked her straight in the eye. I'm meeting up with the guys. Don't wait up. I'm liable to be late. I turned away I'm sure she wanted to argue but I didn't look back. I left her sitting on the side of the bed, she'd be sleep in 10 minutes tops. I was out the door and on my way to Mesha's place in no time. Thoughts of my wife immediately disappeared she had been the warm-up, but Mesha would be the full coarse meal. Mesha was the only one on my mind.

CHAPTER 9

WHAT'S MISSING?

Jennifer: I couldn't pinpoint when I lost him, but Javon was definitely not the man I fell in love with. I tried to rekindle our love on many occasions. Tonight, as I stood there and silently urged him to seduce me when really I hoped I was seducing him. He barely even recognized me. I was desperate. I jumped in front of him and hurriedly sucked his dick against his will. Shit, was that rape? What the fuck ever he's my husband. When I was finished sucking his dick, I pushed him in the chair and jumped on his dick, road that bitch until I was exhausted. Javon picked me up pushed me on the bed face first. My ass was in the air. He fucked me so well I started Cumming all over his dick. I ran a tub and got in, he jumped in the shower. Before he got out the shower I'd completed my bath and put on a new negligee, sat on the side of the bed like I was getting ready to go to sleep. Javon has always been known to take long showers, that's why I'd usually end up taking a bath. We never showered together anymore, even though we have an amazingly huge shower. We used to do some pretty freaky things in our shower back at our old place where the shower stall was so small you would think we were at the local YMCA.

Where are you going? I asked. He shot me a look and said he was going out with the guys, but I already knew the truth. He'd been having an affair. He had to think I was pretty dense if he figured I didn't know. I wasn't ashamed of what happened next. I threw on a coat, straight over my lingerie and grabbed my keys. I followed him to her place. I stayed far enough back, but I didn't shy away from him. I couldn't when this was my marriage we were talking about. I snuck into her house through a side door, the same one my husband had entered just minutes before. My eyes drifted up the stairs where I could already imagine the moaning and groaning. I wasn't going anywhere, I had plenty of time, I knew my husband had a long refractory period so he wouldn't be giving her any dick tonight. I walked into the kitchen and spotted a well-stocked wine cooler under the island, I bypassed the cheap bottle she had on ice and went directly to the 1865 Chateau Lafite, yes this one was nice!

Mesha: He told me I was sexy as if I needed a reason to bring him into my bedroom. We were already in bed, naked and thrashing on top of the covers, within five minutes of him being there. OH GOD... I cried, arching my back, and relishing the feel of his teeth on my nipples, then dragging down to my stomach. His mouth hung at my pussy and he flicked out his tongue, capturing my wetness. I thought he was going to go all oral on me, but he quickly changed things up, put his condom on and was between my thighs about ready to plunge into me, when we heard a cork from a wine bottle pop. We stopped mid-plunge and turned to the right where a woman, now stood holding a bottle of wine, my bottle of wine, my bottle of wine I think. The woman I found out was Jennifer, Javon's wife. I felt him collapse and roll off of me. I was stunned that this was happening to me again. When I mentioned divorce she looked at Javon with curious eyes that told me it was news to her about a divorce. He had lied to me, she knew nothing about a divorce. Javon's bitch ass couldn't even look me in the eye when I said you're getting a divorce right? He'd told me his wife didn't keep herself up and she lacked confidence. Now this woman is standing in my bedroom half naked looking like a Victoria secret model. With my

$4500 bottle of wine in her hand, Jennifer was staring at us. She took a swig and I was stuck on real stupid for a minute, as I set in my bed watching Javon get dress. I finally pulled my robe from the chair beside the bed and put it on. Hardly any words were spoken as he gathered his things and left. That was the last time I saw Javon and I could only imagine the tongue-thrashing he got from his wife. I was over it, heartbroken again, and just angry that I allowed it to happen. I really put my foot down and said that enough was enough. I was not going to fall into this trap again, but…I did. By now you must be thinking I'm dumb as hell! I met Reggie. On the surface, Reggie seemed like the perfect guy, but in all actuality…he was just another married man that wanted to fool me. We didn't even get to the sex before he told me. In fact, I decided I would take things slow with him because I didn't want to fall into another trap. So, on one hand, I was relieved, but on the other, I just kept kicking myself until I realized what I needed. I needed to focus on me and say forget men. I was tired of the same problems and I really meant that.

Gavin: I still couldn't believe I said goodbye to Mesha. It was honestly the toughest decision I ever had to make and even while I snuggle up with Tamia four months after we got married, I question if I did the right thing. I looked over at my beautiful wife. She is everything I have ever desired in a woman. There was only one characteristic she didn't have and that was that she wasn't Mesha. I had to somehow get Mesha out of my mind, but there was a problem with that and it caused a dilemma for me to ponder. I wanted to be with Mesha. I gave her the opportunity for us to be friends and it wasn't for her sake, it was for mine. I didn't expect her to call, but honestly, I wished a little she hadn't. Now, I just had to somehow find a way to have everything I desired…my beautiful wife and Mesha, the woman I could have seen as my future. So, one day when Tamia was out jogging, I went ahead and made the call myself. She didn't answer, as I thought she probably wouldn't, so I left a message. "Hey there, it's Gavin. Just wanted to touch base. It's been a few months, after all, and I hope you're doing really well. Call me back and we can meet up somewhere. I understand if you don't, but I would love it if you would. Talk later." I hung up and stared at my cell. The ball was in her court and I was anxious to see what she'd do.

CHAPTER 10

HE'S BACK

Mesha: I thought I was in a state of depression when Tyrone and I broke up because of his marriage, which was nothing compared to Javon and then Reggie. I only asked for honesty and I was lied to. With Javon, there wasn't a divorce, or at least not one that was around the corner. His wife never said a word, she just turnedm and walked out the door with my wine. With Reggie, he just withheld the truth. I went about my days feeling more and more dejected and then the day came when I saw Gavin was trying to call me. I couldn't deal with him right then. Too much time had passed and my life wasn't any better for it. So, I waited for him to leave the message and then I listened. In his voice, I heard sadness. It wasn't supposed to be what I heard, considering he was married to the love of his life, or so he seemed to think so. But something in his voice told me that I needed to reach out to him and I needed to figure out what was going on. So, I waited two days and called him back. He answered right away and what I got out of it was that he was thrilled I called him. I even felt good about it and I decided to meet up with him. Whether it was a great idea or not, it was what I had to do, because something inside of me said that Gavin needed a friend. We met at a small restaurant that was far enough away from town that no one would see us. When he walked in the door it was as if no time had passed and I wanted to run to him. He smiled. I smiled and the world stood still. How the hell could he still make me feel this way?

Gavin: It was wrong on so many levels that Mesha and I met up because what I found out was that I have been secretly desiring her for way too long. I entered and it was like we were in a romance movie. If love songs could have started playing in the background, it would have been perfect. She came to me and we hugged, we shouldn't have because my body reacted to her in ways that I wanted to react to Tamia. I felt like a fool longing for something that was once mine. Hey, I said. She smiled at me and we went to a table. We talked for hours about everything…about nothing. It just felt good to be there with her and when she said we should part, neither one of us wanted to. Yet, we did, but that didn't last for long. We got back together the next night and then a few nights after that. In the first month, we saw each other twelve times and each time I felt more connected to her than the time before. I even found myself one night telling her I loved her. Her eyes were like saucers and I couldn't take it back. It was the truth. She tried telling me that I didn't mean it, but we both knew that I did. I thought that was the end of our friendship, but I was so wrong.

Mesha: Love was a complicated word and when he said it I wanted to believe that he didn't mean it because that was just easier. Yet, I saw it in his eyes. He loved me and I loved him and that wasn't an easy situation to be in. But I really couldn't change the way I felt and I didn't want to change the way he felt, so I did it. I invited him back to my house in hopes that we could have one night together. Then it hit me that OMG, I was going to have sex with yet another married man. Clearly, something was wrong with me, but I did not even care. I needed to be with him. We got back to my place and we didn't even make it past the living room. Clothes were lying in heaps on the floor and we were snuggling up on the couch. He had already pulled a condom out and it was laying on the arm of the couch, just ready to be used. I wondered down his body and shoved his dick in my mouth, swallowing him whole, and sucking feverishly on his erection. I didn't remember him being so large, but he was. The tip of his penis tickled the back of my throat. I gulped with each thrust. He wiggled between my lips, then pushed his load into my mouth. I ran my tongue in circles, as I felt him tugging at my hair. It was so good to taste him again. His dick plopped out of my mouth and I wondered back up his body, digging my nails into his skin and pulling myself up. We kissed. His hands were clutching my ass and It felt so good being snuggled in his arms that I couldn't imagine not being there, but not everything works as we imagine.

Gavin: I fit so perfectly inside her. It's like we were made for each other, like two connecting pieces of a puzzle. Her body rocked on top of mine and we just explored one another, getting reacquainted and this whole time never once did I think about Tamia. Was that wrong? Uh, yeah…that was awful, but I didn't let it dictate my life. I lived in the moment and in that moment, it was telling me that I had to have sex with Mesha. It was certainly nothing I could personally control. She collapsed against me and we kissed, months of pent up anguish was released. It was out there and I wanted to believe that she would see this as a partnership she wanted to continue. However, I didn't see that right before I left her house she would choose to take a break from what we had going on. You don't even want to be friends? I asked. She shook her head and told me it

would be too hard. It made sense, but wow…I felt really empty

inside. I left her house hoping I would one day see her again, but

knowing that it was a very good possibility I wouldn't

CHAPTER 11

MOVING ON

Mesha: I spent weeks, not days, locked up in my house and bawling over losing Gavin all over again. Tina and none of my other friends could even get to me. I felt like a lost soul. After weeks of wallowing in my pity, I had to get out the house. Besides, there was hardly any food in the house. I looked around grabbed a few essentials, and then stopped off at a small diner. I looked like I hadn't had a shower in weeks. I had, but I did just put on lounge pants and strolled in there with my hair pulled back in a ponytail and that was as much as I did. I placed an order and I ate quietly, expecting to eat and just get out of there. That's when I looked up and noticed that I was being watched. The waitress ask me if I needed anything, I said check please. I was sure that I wasn't seeing things correctly and thinking this guy had to be looking at someone else. When I looked back, he was smiling. He got up from his chair and even walked over to me.

I felt self-conscious, especially because I looked like a hobo. He said hello and I looked up at him. He was handsome, by most people's standards. He had dark curly hair and big gray eyes and he wore a suit and tie, which I found very sexy. I cleared my throat. Hello. My voice was shaky. He asked if he could sit down. I was floored, but immediately offered him the seat and he took it. By habit, my eyes dipped down to his ring finger and he laughed. I quickly looked up, feeling embarrassed. I didn't want to have these thoughts, but they were there. Who was this guy and was he just another married fool?

Lawrence: I saw the look in her eyes as she looked down at my hand. I wondered if she was looking for a ring. What are you looking for? I asked. Sure enough, that was her response. Then she started talking about how men couldn't be trusted and that she was duped too many times and I was staring at her beautiful face in awe and wonderment. She blushed and I melted. I'm not married, I assured her. She didn't even show any sign of relief. I promised her then and said it again. I'm really not married. She then started to relax and we talked. I told her that I was a doctor and new to the area and I could tell that so much pain rose in her eyes. I wanted to do everything I could to take that pain away, but would she let me.

Mesha: I don't mean to be a cynic, I stated quietly. I smiled and he just looked like a genuine person. I found myself really drawn to him and it annoyed me, because what if it was just all lies again. There seemed to be something different about him, though and I figured I would just take things slow. After all, I wasn't a spinster and I wanted to have a true connection, so fingers crossed. Would this finally work out? Only time would tell.

To be continued.

Mesha 2
Find Your Own Man

Chapter 1

Mesha: I decided I needed to take things slow…or at least slower than I usually did. Mainly, because of all the failures I had come across with the married men in my life, I had to be more conscious of what I was doing. So, even though I immediately felt very drawn to Lawrence, I couldn't just open up and let him think that he was getting to me right off. We started just hanging out. I basically said it was just two friends getting together. I wasn't classifying this as a relationship, because let's face it…me and relationships, well, we don't really mix well. So, Lawrence attempted to get me out of my shell and open up more to him, but I was resistant. For the next two weeks, we just hung out. We went to the movies, out for a drink or dinner, or just drove around town so that we were together. Talk about things being anything but romantic. But, it's exactly what I needed. One night, while we were driving around, things did get a little cozier, but that was just after we had been friends for the two weeks. He reached over and touched my knee. In the darkness of the night, I glanced at him and smiled. Hey, I said. He chuckled and without saying anything, he turned back to the road, but his hand remained on my knee. It felt good. It felt relaxing. It felt like I wanted him to touch me in places that he never thought of. We drove a little while longer until he pulled up on top this little hill and parked his car. I turned to him, wondering if this was it and he was going to approach the subject of us being more than just friends. Yet, he didn't.

Lawrence: Ugh! I wanted to kiss this woman so bad. I wanted to prove to her that I was the one man that could make her happy, but every time I even started to say something corny like that, she'd pull back. It was unnerving and did not make me happy. But on this night, with the moon in the background and my hand on her knee, I thought maybe I would be able to gain that courage. Instead, as I parked the car and we stared out into the moonlight, I froze. I asked her to dance. That was all. I turned to her, with the moonlight in her hair, I opened my mouth, and I asked her to dance. She smiled that beautiful smile, the one that always caught me off guard, then nodded. It was a start, but it certainly wasn't the question I wanted to ask her. We got out of the car after I turned the radio on and cranked it up a bit, then walked around the front of the car. It was really romantic. The headlights glistened in the night sky, my arms were around her, and at one point she even put her head on my shoulder. Let's talked about a romantic night that would have been perfect to end with a goodnight kiss or even a night of hot love-making. I looked into her eyes and she beamed back at me like she was telling me it was alright to express my thoughts. I opened my mouth. I really need to ask you a question, I said. I could hear my heart pounding so loud in my ears. I was sure she heard it too.

Mesha: When he said he needed to ask me a question. I swore the question would go something like, *will you have sex with me?* I could have read it in his eyes. That's what he wanted to say. I just know it, but that's not what came out. Instead, Lawrence looked at me and said, there's a party this weekend. A lot of people are going to be there. Wanna come? I felt like the rug was pulled out from underneath my feet. Ummm…sure, I said. He had to have seen the disappointment on my face because, after two weeks of putting him off, I was going to give him a big yes if he would have asked that question. Since he didn't, I could just agree to go with him to the party and be satisfied with that.

Chapter 2

Lawrence: It happened again. I really don't know why I get so tongue-tied around this woman. I opened my mouth to request that we make our relationship official and instead I invited her to a party. It was so lame and I'm surprised she didn't bust out laughing right there. Instead, she just smiled and agreed to go with me. We got back in my car and I took her home. There was no kiss goodnight and no invitation into her place to have sex. So, I needed to get a backbone and take the initiative. After all, the worst thing that could happen is she says no. Well, at least then I would know. So, I picked her up for the party on Saturday night, I needed to show Mesha that I wanted something more than just a friendship with her. You look beautiful, I told her when I picked her up. Figured it was a nice start out to the conversation. She smiled and thanked me, but nothing really much further from there. I drove towards the party with a feeling of just wanting to touch her and be with her. I wondered when my feelings got that strong. I just hoped that I wouldn't lose my nerve by the end of the evening.

Mesha: I was on yet another friendly date with him and all the while I was wondering if tonight would be the night. He never really gave me the indication it would, but I couldn't help thinking about it. At the party, we definitely had motivation. People all around us were dancing and making out and yet, even though at times it seemed like he was on the verge of taking that next step, he just didn't. I was getting frustrated at this point. I'm going to get another drink, I mumbled, hurrying away from him and to the bar that they had set up off to the side of where people were dancing. I needed to escape him, so he wouldn't see my disappointment for another minute. When I got to the bar the bartender walked over to me. What can I get ya, beautiful, he asked. I looked up, surprised to hear some stranger speak those words. My eyes locked on his. His eyes were dark brown and he had a smile that was captivating. I nervously looked away, not expecting to suddenly get turned on by someone that wasn't Lawrence. I'll take a beer on tap, I said. I casually brought my eyes up to his and he was staring right at me. I blushed slightly, then tried to pretend I was interested in looking at something else. He got me my beer and I took a slow drink and thanked him, but even as I left the bar and went back to Lawrence I found that I was drawn to watching him. It was possible I was just sexually deprived and every gorgeous man that stared at me in the way that he stared at me would get my attention, but there was something about those eyes…so familiar…so exciting. I just couldn't stop wanting to turn to look at him. I was so caught up needs.in what was happening at the bar that I didn't even realize Lawrence was calling my name until he touched my arm and I jumped. What? I snapped. He arched an eyebrow and I took a deep breath. I'm sorry, I muttered. I didn't want him to get privy to the idea that I was checking out someone else, while I was supposed to be with him, but I had needs and at the moment Lawrence wasn't fulfilling those

Chapter 3

Lawrence: Ever since she got back from the bar, she was acting strangely. I just sensed this difference in her and I didn't quite understand what it was, but she was almost ignoring me. After we finished our last drinks and I couldn't get past the uncomfortable feeling, I asked her if she wanted to get out of there. She looked at me, almost cutting across as annoyed. I frowned and just watched her mannerisms, but something was definitely off. We did leave the party and when we got outside and reached my car, I turned her around and captured her lips against mine. She was hesitant, fighting it, as she pushed me away. I arched an eyebrow and stared at her. What's going on? I asked. She shrugged and said she was tired. It didn't add up. Here I was finally making my move and yet she seemed to want nothing to do with it. I thought we were doing great. I thought we were on this path, I said. She nodded and looked away. We are, she mumbled. Then, why are you pulling back? I asked. She looked unsure of what to say. I waited, giving her the space she deserved to express herself. I just wanted to know why she was moving backward when I only wanted to move forward.

Mesha: He asked the questions but I couldn't give him the responses he wanted to hear. I couldn't even understand why I was suddenly pulling back. Was it the hot guy at the bar? Was I just confused? Did I even really know what I wanted? The answers to those three questions were the same. I wasn't sure. I wasn't sure why I was finding annoyance in everything he said or did. But, I was certain that my mind kept going back to that bartender and the way he stared at me. I was hooked, so when Lawrence tried to make out with me at the car, I kept finding reasons to turn away. I just don't think this is going to work out, I said. His jaw dropped. Are you kidding me? He asked. I shrugged. It's for the best for both of us. You'll see, I told him. I backed up from him and he reached out to me, even started telling me that if it was because he was going too slow he now knew what he wanted. I wasn't listening to him. I assured him that it wasn't because he was moving too slow. I just needed some space. I meant that because at that very moment I almost felt like I wasn't able to breathe. He asked me to get in the car and we could just talk, but I wasn't even hearing him. I'll call Lyft, I said. I turned around and hurried towards the house, where the party was still in full swing. I didn't know what I was about to do, but I knew that I had to think things through and hope the answer would just miraculously appear.

Lawrence: I stood against the car, expecting that she would come back out and say that she was only kidding, we'd go back to my place, and consummate our relationship. However, as I stayed there and time started passing by, I realized that she wasn't coming back out. I fought the urge to go in there and pull her out. She didn't know anyone and the right thing to do would be just that, but she was strong-willed and she would not appreciate it if I did that, so I respected her wishes. I backed off and I left the party, in hopes that she would come to her senses and give me a call to come back for her. It was up to her, but it was the only thing I could do, no matter how much I wanted to go back.

Chapter 4

Xavier: When I looked up, I was surprised to see her heading back to me. She was by far the most gorgeous creature I'd ever seen. She didn't even make eye contact, but it was like she was on a mission and that mission was to come back to the bar. Well, maybe that was just wishful thinking because the next thing I saw she was on her cell phone and she looked pissed about something. She disconnected the call and shoved her phone back in her pocket, then came to the edge of the bar and just stood there. She was surveying the crowd and didn't seem to look interested in the fact that I was standing right there. Can I get you a drink?" I asked. She turned around and her icy stare softened. She shook her head. No thank you, she replied. She leaned against the bar and her body language cried out for me to keep talking! Excuse me, I stumbled over my words a little. I'm Xavier and you are? She smiled at me, which had me excited. Mesha, she said. I grinned back at her and nodded. Mesha…a beautiful name for a beautiful woman. She blushed and looked away and I had to keep the conversation going. As far as I was concerned, I couldn't let her walk away from me for a second time. I had to learn more about her.

Mesha: I was flirting with him and I didn't care who noticed. Xavier was someone that I wanted to get to know more about and when he opened up the conversation, I let it flow. This is a great party! I said, turning back to him. He nodded. The best, he replied. Our eyes locked in another heated exchange and this time I didn't look away. We continued to talk the all evening and I nearly forgot about my lack of transportation and the fact that every friend I called had other plans. I wasn't looking forward to the taking a lonely Lyft ride by myself, that was for sure, but Xavier made me forget all that. He stepped away only a few times to gather drinks for other guests at the party and I just stood and watched him. He always returned to me, with a smile and an another easy exchange in conversation. As the night pressed on, I lost track of time. He made it easy to forget about everything else going on around us. When he paused and got all serious, I was amazed by his words. You have beautiful eyes, he said. I smiled, wanting to pass along a conversation to him, too. Thank you and you have a gorgeous smile. He laughed and nodded.

Thank you, he replied back. I could stare at that smile all night and as it turned out, that's pretty much what happened. Before I knew it, he had to start packing up his things and cleaning up. I nervously looked around, remembering that I had to get a ride still. I dug my phone back out of my pocket and dialed up Tina's number.

Chapter 5

Tina: I yawned as I tried to focus my attention on her call. I looked over at the clock on the nightstand and my eyes bugged out. Mesha, it's after two, I complained. I had a late night myself but even with that being said, I was in bed before midnight. I'm fully aware, Mesha said. So, can you come pick me up? She continued. I tossed my head back, releasing another yawn. It was overly loud and I apologized for that, hearing Mesha sigh on the other end. I'm sorry for bothering you, Tina, she said. I'll get someone else. You're tired. I groaned at Mesha's words, then remembered that she was going out with Lawrence. What happened to Lawrence? I asked. She groaned. I didn't like the sound of that. She was always saying good things about him because they were going slow, despite the fact that this wasn't usually her style. What's wrong? I asked. She told me nothing, but I could sense she was hiding something. I opened my mouth to tell her that I would be right there when I heard a guy on the other end and Mesha told me to hold on. I frowned and waited as the two of them carried on a conversation. I was about to burst out and ask Mesha what was going on when she came back on the phone. Never mind, Tina. I have a ride, she said. I thought about those words. Who's the guy? I asked. She was very vague, basically telling me he was some random guy she just met and I couldn't believe she was convincing me that she would be alright getting a ride home with him. Don't be silly, I'm on my way, I said. However, she immediately stopped me. I'll be fine, she told me, then disconnected the phone. I laid in bed and knew that I would worry until I heard from her again. I wondered who the guy was and why Lawrence wasn't in the picture.

Mesha: Ready to get out of here? He asked me. I nodded, still finding it hard to believe that when he offered me the ride I found I didn't want to say no. We got outside and when we reached a parking lot I saw there were only a few vehicles. I looked up at him. Which one are you? I asked. He grinned and pointed to the motorcycle that was between two cars. I had a thing for the bad boys, that was obvious to most. He walked over and handed me his helmet. I put it on, feeling all excited to be on the back of his bike.

He got on, then pulled me on behind him. Where are we headed? He called out to me. I smiled, feeling like that was an open invitation. Wherever the road takes us, I said. He grinned and nodded, then started his bike. The one thing I knew, I didn't want the morning to end without really getting to know this man. I didn't care where we went.

Xavier: The feel of her arms around me got me carried away. I knew exactly where I wanted to take her. I drove through the empty streets, heading down several back roads until we were coming to a clearing of an open field. I stopped on the side of the road, then helped her down from the bike. I slowly helped her with her helmet and found she was grinning from ear to ear. She looked around. Where are we? She asked, then her eyes found mine. Lookout Ridge, I answered. I opened up the case on the back of my bike and pulled out a blanket. You've never been? I asked. A bit surprised, I had to admit. She shook her head and I motioned for her to follow me. There's an amazing view over here and you can be as LOUD as you WANT to. I laughed as I yelled out part of the words. I glance at her she was chuckling. There won't be a soul around, I concluded. We continued until we came across the farthest point West and I laid out the blanket and motioned for her to sit down. When she did, she looked straight up and I joined her. The full moon was cascading over the night sky and if you were quiet you could hear the breeze of the air echoing across the field. Amazing, she mumbled. I looked over at her and got caught up by her beauty. Absolutely breathtaking, I said. I was speaking of her, of course, and when she turned to look at me, she could tell. She smiled and then looked back up at the moon. I watched her until I didn't want to make her feel awkward, then looked back up at the sky. It was a clear night with a million stars in the sky and I only had eyes for her.

Chapter 6

Mesha: I'd never met anyone like him. He seemed like the bad boy that was a little rough around the edges, bartender, someone you should keep your daughters away from. However, the truth was...he was far from it. He was sweet, kind, and in the time that I met him, I saw he was also smart and a hopeless romantic. It was going on three in the morning and we were out looking at the stars and just enjoying the peace and quiet. I would casually glance in his direction and he would be staring at me or smiling while he looked up at the stars and pointed out another member of the Galaxy family. I wasn't even tired. When he was through with showing me the road map of the constellations, he turned back to me. I was certain he would say it was time to get me home. However, that seemed to be the furthest thing from his mind. He moved in closer to me and touched my cheek, whipping a strand of hair behind my ear. I smiled at him and he leaned in and kissed me. It started off very sweet and then turned a little more sensual. He slid his tongue over my lower lip, causing a moan to escape me and then he lowered me to the blanket. A

million thoughts went through my mind. I was back to moving too

quickly with a man. I should take things slower and just let a

relationship build, but my thoughts were shoved out as he started to

pull my shirt off over my head and I worked on undressing him.

Who cares if we were developing this too fast? I just wanted to be

with him, I'd have to deal with my conscience later.

Chapter 7

Xavier. The last piece of clothing was shed and I rolled a condom onto my throbbing manhood. The cool night air was blowing softly over our bodies, making the intensity and longing for her, even that much greater. I straddled her body, letting my cock slowly move into her and then wrapped my arms around her. My lips went to hers and we kissed while rocking our bodies against one another. I had mentioned she could be as loud as she wanted and she was. She shrieked into the night, which our hips crashed against one another, overpowering the emotions inside of me. I took my lips back to hers and thrust my tongue down her throat, showing her that I was in the moment and right where I wanted to be. Since meeting her, I couldn't tear my eyes away, since touching her…I couldn't let the feeling go. My cock expanded inside of her as I plunged deeper into her folds, opening her up and causing her to spasm around me. The sensation was out of this world and I plowed into her with persistence and drive. She shook under me, parting from the kiss and gasping for air, as I slid my lips to her breasts and started to kiss them, along with flipping my tongue across her nipples. She shivered

and I lowered myself and began lavishing her breasts with my lips. I

held onto her waist as I slowed my movements. I let out a grunt and

collapsed on top of her, while my body came down from my own

orgasm. I softly kissed her shoulder as I held her in my arms. If I

could be anywhere at that moment, I would still want to be there. I

pulled up and looked into her eyes. We then laughed and collapsed

against one another. She felt the same way, too. I fell down next to

her and we drifted off to sleep, holding one another, and wondering

if more was to come.

Chapter 8

Tina: I don't know where you are, Mesha, and why you're not answering your phone, but you better pick up quick or I'm going to send the cops out looking for you. I hung up the phone as I tried Mesha one more time. I hadn't heard from her since two o'clock that morning and it was now noon. I thought for sure she would have at least picked up the phone and called to tell me she was alive. I was furious and seriously only giving her an hour to make the call and get me back in the loop. I sat by the phone and waited and waited and waited some more. It was about five minutes until the hour when I heard my phone and quickly glanced at it. Upon seeing Mesha's name, I answered it. Where've you been? I've been worried sick, Tina yelled. Mesha just laughed on the other end. I'm sorry, she apologized. This is the first chance I've had to call you. I never wanted you to worry. She then hesitated and when she spoke again, I would have fallen over if I wasn't sitting down. I met someone, she said. What? I asked, confused by the sudden outburst. She then told me about this guy named Xavier and how he seemed different and I was still unable to comprehend the words she spoke. I could only utter three words. Just be careful, I said. She laughed off my genuine concern, but I had seen her hurt so many times, that I didn't want to see that happen again. We talked a little more, mainly about how special he made her feel. When we got off the phone I felt like maybe he could be different. I just could only hope he was.

Mesha: Things were different with Xavier than they were with Lawrence. With Lawrence, things started off slow and then started to build up until I forced it to fizzle out. With Xavier, things started strong and kept growing even stronger. In a few short weeks, we were spending every waking minute together. When he would have to go to work, then we would part, but that was about the extent of things. Either he would stay over at my place or I would stay over at his. When I woke up in his arms, I felt loved but it wasn't until we had officially been together for a month, did he tell me that he loved me. He was getting ready for work and turned to me. I wish I could stay with you tonight, Mesha, he said. I knew what he meant. It was technically our month anniversary, but in my opinion, we would have

plenty of anniversaries together, so it didn't matter. Then he said it.

I love you, Mesha. I smiled, feeling my heart fluttering in my chest.

And I love you, I said, leaning in and kissing him. The kiss deepened

and I could have ripped his clothes off right then, but he couldn't

miss work. I parted from the kiss. Now, go to work and when you

get back I'll properly show you just how much. He groaned but

nodded and I said goodbye to him and watched him leave my

apartment. I grinned and twirled around in my living room. Saying

the three words to him was something I felt deep within my heart

and I couldn't be happier.

Chapter 9

Gavin: I stared at my phone as Tamia's words echoed through my mind. *Am I no longer attractive to you?* She asked. I swallowed the growing lump in my throat. It wasn't exactly that. I found that my attraction didn't disappear for my wife, but there were moments when I couldn't help but think about another woman in my life and wonder what she was up to. It'd been a couple months since I'd been with Mesha, but not a day went by that I didn't think about her and slowly Tamia seemed to realize something was off. *I don't know what's wrong,* I tried telling her. I couldn't tell her the truth because that would only bring heartache, but not being able to give her a definitive answer, had her walking out the door. Her last words to me that night were *until you figure you out, I'm going to stay with a friend.* She slammed the door behind her and I just let her go.

That was last night and now tonight I'm stuck sitting here and thinking about how I wanted to talk to Mesha. I tossed the phone down, discouraged and frustrated. I was still a married man and calling Mesha would only complicate things. I stood up from the couch and started

pacing. I kept looking at the phone and imagining how it would be to talk to her again. Yet, knowing that if I took that step, then my marriage could be over forever.

Chapter 10

Mesha: Saying goodbye to Xavier only got more difficult as time wore on in our relationship. But tonight it seemed impossible. A whole weekend? I asked him. He chuckled. You'll be fine, but duty calls. He told me of a job he took that was in another town he was going for orientation this weekend so he can start work on Monday. It wouldn't pay for him to drive back and forth, we could visit one another he was looking for an apartment there. As I stood at the door saying goodbye to him, I felt emptiness. I brushed my hand against his face and stared up at him. How did I fall so hopelessly in love with this man? It'd been awhile since I had such a connection. I'll miss you! I whispered. He smiled. I'll miss you more. I shook my head. Impossible, I mumbled. I kissed him once more, then had to shoo him away, before I caught myself not letting him go. He picked up his bag and opened up the door. I love you, he said. I love you, I answered back. Then he was gone. I closed the door behind him, then fell back against the door and silently willed for him to come back. That's when there was a knock at the door. I grinned

and tossed the door open. Did you... I caught myself before I could

finish that sentence. Gavin? I asked. He grinned and moved closer

to me. Hello, Mesha. May I come in? I couldn't even fully

comprehend he was there as I stared into his eyes and for a

second...I was lost, why the hell was he here?

To be continued.

B ehind him, headlights flashed, rose up into the trees. Tires crunched over gravel. The car stopped, its motor still ticking.

Zach turned.

Crap.

Black caddy. New dent in the back. And tall, dark and gruesome stepped out of the car: Dennis, Cat's menace.

Crap. Crap. Crap.

Silently, the chauffer glided toward Zach. Grinning, displaying a shark's worth of white teeth.

EZ Brite goes on quick, tastes so good, just give it a lick...

No! Focus!

Zach swept up Samantha in one arm, wielding the filled diaper in the other hand. "Get back! I've got a diaper! And I'm not afraid to use it."

The chauffer stopped. Zach met his pale blue gaze, standing his ground. Then the tall man grabbed Zach's arm and squeezed, a show of strength. "You're coming with me."

"Dude, get off me!" Zach shrugged him loose, whirled. Brought up the diaper.

Splat. A perfect landing.

Stunned, Dennis staggered back, his hands clawing at his face.

Screaming as if he'd been burned. Only far worse.

The chauffer rebounded, reeled back, swung. Zach ducked, Samantha tucked against his belly. A double punch whooshed over Zach's head.

Zach danced back, a boxer's taunt. He planted the ball of his foot, pivoted, kicked the other leg up. Rolling it out kick boxer style. Part of his rigid dancing training.

His foot caught the much larger man in the chest. Dennis stumbled backward, arms flailing for balance. Gravity won the day, dropping him to the cement. Zach seized the moment, ran at him with Samantha cradled in his arms like a football. He leaped. Another kick to the chauffer's face, one for the road. He went flat on his back, out.